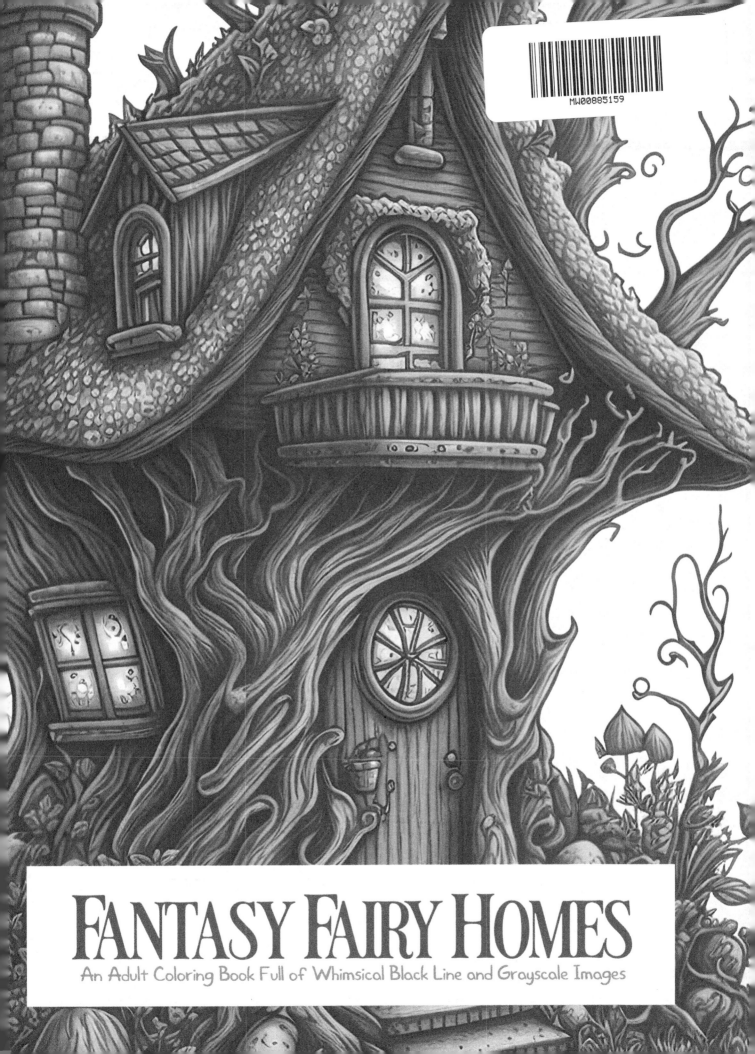

FANTASY FAIRY HOMES

An Adult Coloring Book Full of Whimsical Black Line and Grayscale Images

Thank you for choosing our coloring book and supporting our small business!

We hope you have fun coloring! Everyone who contributed to this book appreciates your support.

Please leave a review and share some of your beautiful colored pictures on our amazon page.

You can find us at:
amazon.com/author/clairessa

Scan our QR code to join our mailing list at:
www.clairessa.club

Be the first to know about new coloring book releases and alerted when we release our
MONTHLY FREE PRINTABLE
MINI COLORING BOOK!

TO ACCESS YOUR MONTHLY FREE MINI COLORING BOOK

1) Search "Clair Essa Coloring" or visit: www.clairessa.club

2) Go to FREE BOOK

3) Click DOWNLOAD

4) Print and enjoy!

COLORING TIPS & TRICKS

1) Our paper is most suited for colored pencils, crayons, pastels, and alcohol-based markers. Experiment with different shading techniques and textures to create your own unique style!

2) In addition to being a great stress-reducer and relaxation activity, coloring can also be a fun way to connect with others. Share your finished pages on social media with the hashtag #clairessacoloring!

3) To protect upcoming pages, we recommend placing a blank piece of paper under the page you're working on.

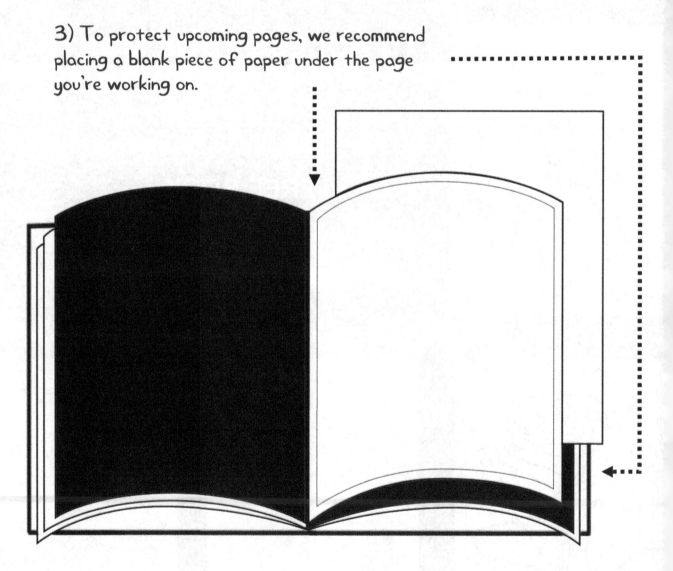

THIS BOOK BELONGS TO:

_____

Congratulations on finishing the book! We hope you had a great time coloring!

Your reviews help us immensely and help others find our books! Please consider leaving a review on Amazon.

You can find our books at:
amazon.com/author/clairessa

And remember to visit, **www.clairessa.club**, for your MONTHLY FREE PRINTABLE COLORING BOOK!

We add a new free book every month! Join our mailing list to stay in the loop.

Use our QR code for
quick access!

Want more to color? Check out our best sellers:

Made in the USA
Coppell, TX
31 January 2024

28434185R10050